Ocean Explorers

Essex County Council

'Ocean Explorers'
An original concept by Katie Dale
© Katie Dale 2025

Illustrated by Ronaldo Barata

Published by MAVERICK ARTS PUBLISHING LTD

Suite 1, Hillreed House, 54 Queen Street,

Horsham, West Sussex, RH13 5AD

© Maverick Arts Publishing Limited May 2025

+44 (0)1403 256941

A CIP catalogue record for this book is available at the British Library.

ISBN 978-1-83511-058-4

Printed in India

www.maverickbooks.co.uk

Ocean Explorers

Written by
Katie Dale

Illustrated by
Ronaldo Barata

Chapter 1

As the school bell rang, Finn grabbed his bag and raced outside, beaming as brightly as the summer sunshine. It was finally the school holidays!

"Are you going away?" his friend Max asked. "I can't wait to spend two weeks on a hot, sunny beach!"

"My parents are working, so I'm staying with my Aunt Lucy and Uncle Jim," Finn replied. "We're going somewhere where it's dark and cold and there's barely *any* sunshine at all!"

"Ugh!" Max grimaced. "Poor you! That sounds **horrible!**"

But Finn laughed. "I can't wait!"

Finn's skin tingled with excitement. Every year, he had begged his parents to let him go exploring the oceans with his aunt and uncle, and now he couldn't believe he was actually, finally, on a real-life submarine!

"I'm so glad you could join us this summer, Finn," Aunt Lucy smiled. "Especially as this will be our last trip."

"Your last trip?" Finn frowned. "Why?"

"The expeditions are expensive," Uncle Jim sighed. "And I'm afraid our funding has run out."

"So we'll just have to make this the best trip ever!" Aunt Lucy said, hugging Finn. "Just look at that view!"

"I've never seen such incredible fish and animals!" Finn gasped as he gazed out of the window.

"There might be creatures down here that *nobody* has ever seen before!" Kara added, smiling. "Can you believe that over 70 percent of the Earth is covered in ocean, but only 10 percent of the oceans have been explored?! Who knows what hidden treasures we'll discover!"

"Let me show you around the sub," Uncle Jim grinned.

The tour didn't take long. By the time Finn had seen the engine room, the bunk beds and the galley (which is what they called the submarine kitchen), there was only one room left—the Tiddler HQ. Inside was a console with what looked like a virtual reality headset and controllers. There was also a tablet.

"This is where we control the Tiddler!" Uncle Jim said. "It's a remote-control submersible attached to the sub. We use it to get a better look at things the sub is too big to get close to. Would you like to try it, Finn?" he winked.

"Really?" Finn said eagerly. **"Yes please!"**

Tom helped Finn put on the headset. Instantly, Finn could see fish and coral all around him.

"Use the controllers to travel around," Uncle Jim said, watching on the tablet. "Watch out for the coral!" Finn slowly moved the controller and immediately felt like he was moving. Shoals of tiny fish shimmered as they swam out of his way. It felt like he was actually swimming underwater—without getting wet!

Chapter 2

Tiddler squeezed into the cave just in time!

"Phew!" Finn sighed as the whales swam past. Luckily, they were too big to follow it into the cave. "That was close! But why did they chase the Tiddler? Were they trying to eat it?"

"Well, they are the world's largest toothed predators…" Tom said.

Finn gulped.

"But it's unlikely they'd try to eat a submersible!" Kara scoffed. "The mother whale had probably never seen one before. She must have worried that it was a threat to her baby. I think she was just trying to scare it away."

"Well, it worked!" Finn laughed nervously.

"She's certainly thrown us off our planned route," Aunt Lucy said. "But then I guess that's what exploring is all about! Finding new places where no one's been before!"

Finn frowned. "Are you sure no one's been here before?"

"Not according to my research," Aunt Lucy replied. "Why?"

"Because someone must have dropped that!" Finn cried, pointing at the screen as Tiddler emerged from the cave into a large open cavern.

Everyone turned to see what he was looking at, then gasped. It was a shoe!

"Well how did that get there?" Uncle Jim chuckled. "We're miles away from land!"

"And we're in the 21st century," Aunt Lucy added. "No one's worn shoes like that for centuries…"

"Look—there's more!" Kara cried as Tiddler passed a hat and a fork. "Where did they all come from?"

But as Tiddler turned, the answer suddenly became crystal clear.

"But... does that mean no one can have the treasure?" Finn frowned. "But then we won't be able to use it to fund your future trips..."

"This is a brand-new species, Finn. It's possibly the only nest on the planet, and we're the very first people to find them," Aunt Lucy replied, beaming at him. "That is much more valuable than any treasure or future expeditions!"

Finn grinned. She was right.

"And you should choose a name for them, Finn," Kara added. "After all, you spotted them first!"

"Really?!" Finn gasped. "Wow! I think I'll call them... Spiny Spikefish!"

Kara laughed. "Perfect!"

"I told you this would be the best trip ever," Aunt Lucy grinned.

Finn beamed. She was right!

But just then...

"Quick!" Tom yelled, running in. "Everyone to the engine room—we're **LEAKING!**"

Chapter 3

Finn's heart pounded in panic as everyone hurried to the engine room. **A leak? On a submarine?!** That was bad—*really bad!* It's not like they could even bail the water out like you would on a normal ship; they were surrounded by water! Even Aunt Lucy, who was normally super-calm, looked worried as they all crowded into the tiny engine room.

"Where's the leak?" Uncle Jim asked, looking around urgently.

Finn looked around too. But, to his surprise, he couldn't see a leak anywhere. There was no sign of water at all.

Then, to his even greater surprise...

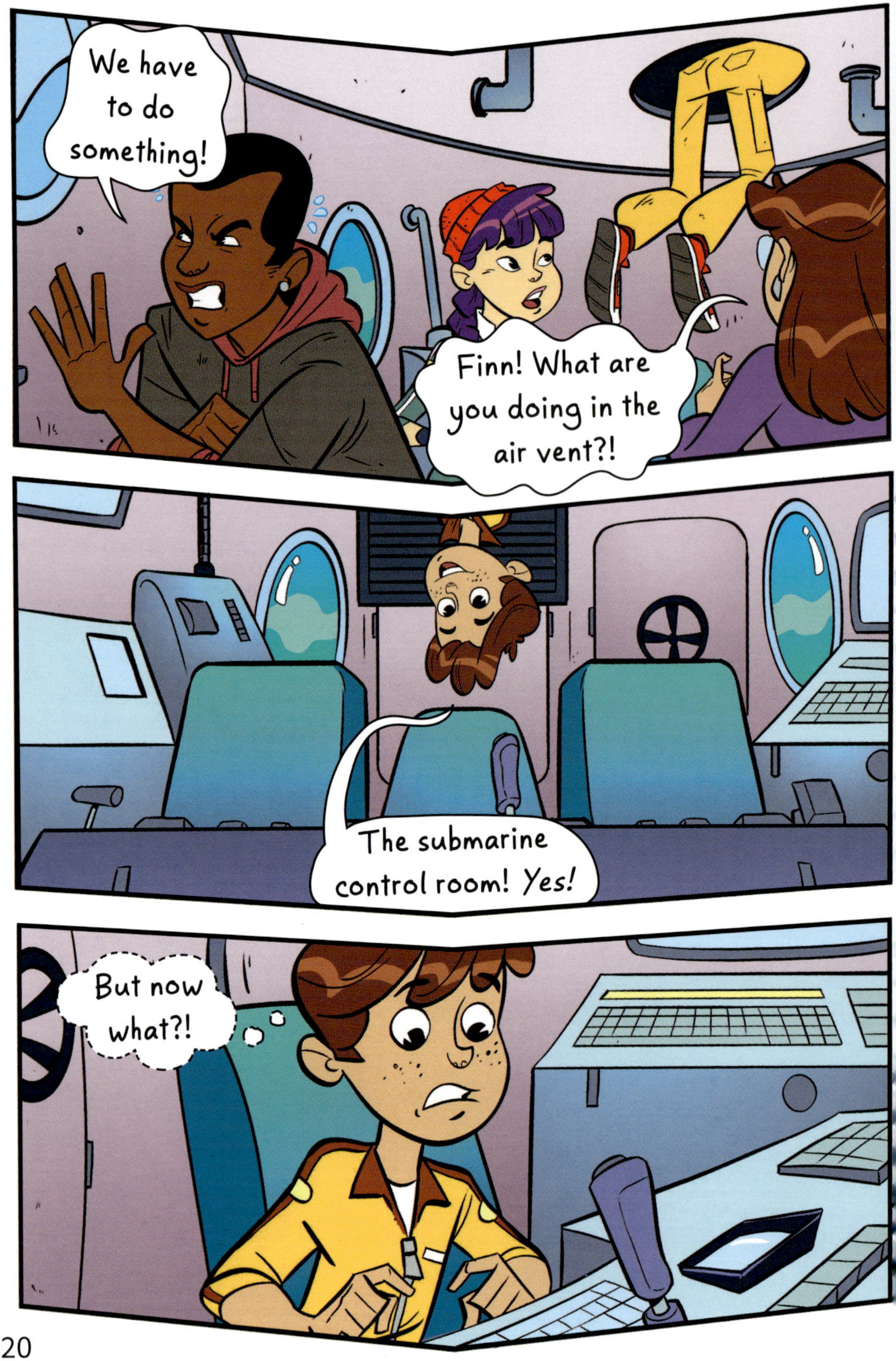

Finn stared at all the buttons and levers helplessly. He had no idea how to control a submarine! One wrong button and he could make everything ten times worse! What if he accidentally turned off the oxygen? Or crashed the sub into the shipwreck? Oh why hadn't he asked his uncle and aunt before he'd left them?! Maybe he should go back and ask? But there wasn't time!

Through the window, he saw Tiddler filling its storage compartment with gold, getting closer and closer to the precious nest. He couldn't believe Tom could be so selfish—how could he risk wiping out an entire species just to get rich? He had to stop him! But how?

Suddenly, Finn's gaze fell on the only lever he'd seen Aunt Lucy use—lights on/off. Could that help? He had to try. After all, if Tom couldn't see the gold, he couldn't steal it, right? Finn pulled the lever, and immediately, the submarine and the wreck were plunged into darkness.

Finn heard Tom's footsteps clanking towards the control room. He had to hide—**QUICK!**

Chapter 4

Finn quickly wriggled his way back through the air vent to the engine room, just as Tom unlocked the door!

"Who turned off the lights?!" Tom demanded, glaring round at them all. Then he frowned. "You're... all still here?"

"Of course!" Uncle Jim snapped. "You locked us in!"

THEN WHO TURNED OUT THE LIGHTS?" Tom said, turning pale.

"Are you alright, Tom?" Kara said. "You look like you've seen a ghost!"

Tom gulped and Finn grinned. Of course! Tom was scared of ghosts! That's how they could scare him away from the nest—just like the whale scared Tiddler away from her baby!

"Is th-this your g-gold?" Tom stammered.

Finn made the lights flash again.

"I-if I leave it here... will you let m-me leave too?"

Finn flashed the lights again.

Tom immediately returned all the gold, and Finn grinned and turned the lights back on.

Tom blinked in the sudden brightness, then brought Tiddler swiftly back to the main sub. Finn hurriedly scrambled back into the air vent and crawled back to the engine room—just in time!

"I'm so sorry!" Tom said, letting everyone out. "I've m-made a huge m-mistake. L-let's go b-back to shore—quickly!"

"Good idea," Aunt Lucy said winking at Finn behind Tom's back.

Finn beamed.

They'd done it! They'd saved the Spiny Spikefish!

Chapter 5

As the submarine sailed away from the shipwreck and back towards the shore, Finn watched the underwater world in wonder. He felt amazed that they'd found a brand-new species, thrilled that he'd been allowed to name them, relieved that he'd been able to save them, but also now rather sad that he'd never see them again.

"I'm so glad we found the Spiny Spikefish when you were with us, Finn," Aunt Lucy said, hugging him. "What an adventure!"

Finn smiled, then frowned. "But won't you miss all your underwater adventures? What will you both do now?"

"A family discovery!" a man with a video camera cried, pushing to the front of the crowd. "How fantastic! What a story! Thanks for the tip, Kara!"

"This is my friend, Mike," Kara smiled, introducing them. "He's a documentary maker."

Finn beamed. Were they going to be famous? What an amazing end to their underwater adventure!

"Great to meet you!" Mike beamed, shaking their hands. "Tell me, where did you find the Spiny Spikefish?"

"They were nesting in a shipwreck in an underwater cavern!" Finn told him excitedly.

Mike's eyes widened. "Nesting? Shipwreck? Underwater cavern? This is incredible! Can you take me there on your submarine to film it? I'd love to make a documentary about the discovery!"

"Unfortunately not," Uncle Jim sighed. "That was our last expedition."

"I'm afraid we don't have the funds for another trip," Aunt Lucy explained.

"My dears, if you take me on your submarine to film my documentary, my production company will pay for everything!" Mike beamed. "What do you say?"

Uncle Jim and Aunt Lucy looked at each other, stunned.

"Well... we do have room for one more crew member, now that Tom's gone..." Uncle Jim said, watching the police take Tom away.

"And it would be wonderful to study the Spiny Spikefish and find out more about them!" Aunt Lucy said excitedly. "With Kara, of course."

"Of course!" Mike cried, beaming at Kara. "So... do we have a deal?"

"It's up to Finn," Aunt Lucy said.

Uncle Jim nodded. "This is your summer with us, Finn," he said. "We'd quite understand if you'd prefer to go back to dry land for the rest of the holidays."

Finn bit his lip. "You mean a summer of sun, sand and safety?" Finn said. "Away from dangerous giant underwater predators, thieves and haunted shipwrecks?"

WHAT NEXT?

Did you enjoy this Fusion Reader? If you are looking for more, the Maverick Reading Scheme is a bright, attractive range of books with plenty of stories for everyone.

MAVERICK FUSION READERS

To view the whole Maverick Reading Scheme, visit our website at www.maverickearlyreaders.com

Or scan the QR code to view our scheme instantly!